The Fisherman and the Turtle

ADAPTED BY **Eric A. Kimmel**

ILLUSTRATED BY **Martha Aviles**

MARSHALL CAVENDISH CHILDREN

Marshall Cavendish Corporation, 99 White Plains Road, Tarrytown, NY 10591
www.marshallcavendish.us/kids

Library of Congress Cataloging-in-Publication Data
Kimmel, Eric A.
The fisherman and the turtle / adapted by Eric A. Kimmel; illustrated by Martha Aviles.— 1st ed.
p. cm.
Summary: A retelling of the Grimm tale about the fisherman's greedy wife, set in the land of the Aztecs.
ISBN 978-0-7614-5387-1
[1. Fairy tales. 2. Folklore—Germany.] I. Avilis Junco, Martha, ill. II. Grimm, Jacob, 1785-1863. III.
Grimm, Wilhelm, 1786-1859. IV. Fisherman and his wife. English. V. Title.
PZ8.K527Fi 2008
398.2—dc22
[E]
2007011710
The text of this book is set in Aged.
The illustrations were rendered in acrylics and liquid watercolor on Arches paper (cotton 300g).
Book design by Becky Terhune
Editor: Margery Cuyler

Printed in Malaysia
First edition
1 3 5 6 4 2

Marshall Cavendish
Children

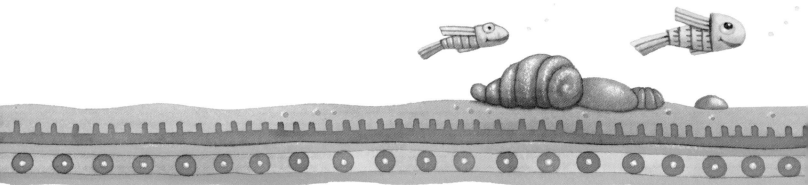

For Diana and Lisa
—E. A. K.

For Miguel, with love
—M. A.

Long ago in the days of the Aztecs, a fisherman and his wife lived in a hut by the seashore.

Every morning the fisherman paddled his boat out to sea. If he caught a fish, he and his wife ate it together. If he caught two fish, they each had one. If he caught three fish, his wife took one to the market and traded it for corn, beans, and chili peppers. Then they made the other two into fish stew for dinner.

And if he caught four fish—well, why bother to speak of that? It never happened.

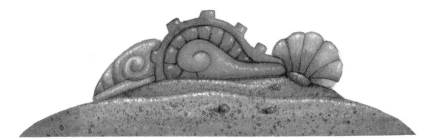

One morning the fisherman cast his net as he always did. As he pulled it up, he felt something heavy in it. It was a green sea turtle.

The turtle spoke. "Fisherman! I am no ordinary turtle. I am one of the seven sons of Opochtli, god of the sea. Spare my life and I will grant you a wish."

What should I wish for? the fisherman wondered. "I know!" he said. "Give me four fish. I have never had a catch like that."

"It is done," the turtle said. He disappeared beneath the waves, leaving four fine fish flapping about the boat.

The fisherman paddled home. "It has been a good day," he told his wife. "I caught a turtle who granted me a wish." He then explained about the four fish. Instead of being pleased, his wife flew into a rage.

"You foolish man! That turtle would have given you anything you wished for. Instead, you asked for four stinking fish. Go back to the sea. Find the turtle. Tell him I am tired of living in a hut. I want a stone house. I want to be rich."

The fisherman paddled out to sea the next morning. He cupped his hands to his mouth and called in a loud voice:

> *Turtle living in the sea,*
> *son of great Opochtli,*
> *my angry wife has made a wish.*
> *She wants more than four fine fish.*

The turtle raised his head above the waves. "What more does she want?"

"She wants to live in a stone house. She wants to be rich," the fisherman said.

"Go home. It is done," the turtle said.

The fisherman paddled home. When he arrived, he saw a great stone house surrounded by fields and gardens standing where the hut had been. His wife came out to greet him. She wore a dress of colorful woven cloth. Gold rings hung from her ears. Flowers perfumed her hair.

"Wife, are we rich?" the fisherman asked.

"Yes, we are," said his wife.

"Are you happy?"

She answered, "For now."

Indeed, they were rich, and for a while, they were happy. Then one day the fisherman's wife came to him and said, "Go back to the sea. Find the turtle. Being rich is not enough. I have wealth. Now I want power. Tell the turtle I want to be king."

The fisherman could not believe his ears. "How can you be king? There is only one king in the land of the Aztecs. He lives far away in the city of Tenochtitlán. The turtle can do many things, but he cannot do that. He cannot make you king."

"How do you know?" his wife asked. "Go ask him."

The fisherman paddled out to sea again. Stormy waves tossed his boat up and down. The wind howled. Salt spray stung his face. The fisherman cupped his hands to his mouth. His voice rang out over the sea.

Turtle living in the sea,
son of great Opochtli,
my angry wife has made me groan.
She wants more than a house of stone.

The turtle raised his head above the waves. "What more does she want?"
"She wants to be king," the fisherman said.
The turtle answered, "Go home. It is done."

The fisherman paddled home. He found the great stone house deserted.

"Where is my wife?" he asked the servants.

"The great lords of the Aztecs came. They took her to the city of Tenochtitlán," they told him. "She is king now."

The fisherman walked to the great city. When he arrived, he stood there amazed, staring at the wide avenues, the flowing canals, the colorful gardens, and the towering temples and palaces.

He made his way to the House of the King. There he saw his wife seated on a carved throne, her wrists and neck encircled with bracelets and necklaces of gold and jade, a crown of quetzal feathers on her head.

"Wife, are you king?" the fisherman asked.

His wife answered, "Yes, I am king."

"And are you happy?"

"For now," she said.

And she was happy. For a time.

Then one morning she summoned the fisherman and said, "Being king is good, but being a god is better. Go back to the turtle. Tell him I want to be one of the gods."

"I cannot do that," the fisherman said, trembling. "The turtle can make you king, but he cannot make you a god."

His wife raged. "Do you forget to whom you speak? I may be your wife, but I am also the king. I do not ask. I command! Go to the turtle. Tell him I want to be a god."

The fisherman had no choice but to obey. He returned to the seashore. Finding his boat, he paddled far out to sea. Never had he seen such a storm. Ferocious winds whipped the black water into an ugly froth. Terrified, the fisherman cupped his hands to his mouth and cried out over the hurricane's roar:

> *Turtle living in the sea,*
> *son of great Opochtli,*
> *my angry wife has made a vow.*
> *She wants more than she has now.*

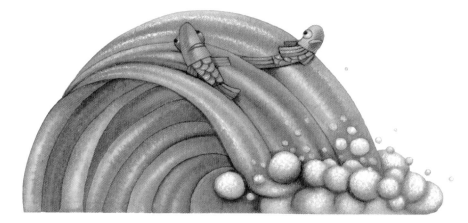

The turtle lifted his head above the towering waves. "She is king. What more can she want?"

"She wants to be one of the gods," the fisherman said.

"And what do you want?" the turtle asked.

"I want to go home," the fisherman said. "I want to go back to my hut. I want my wife to stop asking for more, more, more!"

"Go home. It is done," the turtle said.

The fisherman closed his eyes. When he opened them, he found himself back on the seashore. He saw his wife seated on a jade throne beside their hut. She held a bowl of cornmeal in her lap. Garlands of flowers hung around her neck.

"Are you happy now?" the fisherman asked.

But his wife never answered. The turtle indeed had granted her wish. She had become like all the other gods in Tenochtitlán. A statue carved from stone.

Centuries have passed. The hut and the Aztecs are gone. The great city of Tenochtitlán is only a memory. But the great turtle still swims in the sea, as he has since the beginning of time.

If you met him, what would you wish for?

The Fisherman and the Turtle is set in the days of the Aztec empire of Mexico. It is based on the well-known tale "The Fisherman and His Wife" (*Von dem Fischer un syner Fru*) from Grimms' Fairy Tales. I also incorporated elements from "The Crown of Sang Nila Utama," a story from Singapore with a similar theme. As the saying goes, "Be careful with wishes. They might come true."

—Eric A. Kimmel